Dear Parent:

Congratulations! Your child is taking the first steps on an exciting journey. The destination? Independent reading!

STEP INTO READING® will help your child get there. The program offers five steps to reading success. Each step includes fun stories and colorful art. There are also Step into Reading Sticker Books, Step into Reading Math Readers, Step into Reading Write-In Readers, Step into Reading Phonics Readers, and Step into Reading Phonics First Steps! Boxed Sets—a complete literacy program with something for every child.

Learning to Read, Step by Step!

Ready to Read   Preschool–Kindergarten
• big type and easy words • rhyme and rhythm • picture clues
For children who know the alphabet and are eager to begin reading.

Reading with Help   Preschool–Grade 1
• basic vocabulary • short sentences • simple stories
For children who recognize familiar words and sound out new words with help.

Reading on Your Own   Grades 1–3
• engaging characters • easy-to-follow plots • popular topics
For children who are ready to read on their own.

Reading Paragraphs   Grades 2–3
• challenging vocabulary • short paragraphs • exciting stories
For newly independent readers who read simple sentences with confidence.

Ready for Chapters   Grades 2–4
• chapters • longer paragraphs • full-color art
For children who want to take the plunge into chapter books but still like colorful pictures.

STEP INTO READING® is designed to give every child a successful reading experience. The grade levels are only guides. Children can progress through the steps at their own speed, developing confidence in their reading, no matter what their grade.

Remember, a lifetime love of reading starts with a single step!

To Terry, who loves to dance
—S.L. & M.L.

Text copyright © 1998 by Sally Lucas. Illustrations copyright © 1998 by Margeaux Lucas. All rights reserved under International and Pan-American Copyright Conventions. Published in the United States by Random House Children's Books, a division of Random House, Inc., New York, and simultaneously in Canada by Random House of Canada Limited, Toronto. Originally published by Golden Books, an imprint of Random House Children's Books, a division of Random House, Inc., in 1998.

www.stepintoreading.com

Educators and librarians, for a variety of teaching tools, visit us at www.randomhouse.com/teachers

Library of Congress Cataloging-in-Publication Data:
Lucas, Sally, 1933– .
Dancing dinos / by Sally Lucas ; illustrated by Margeaux Lucas.
    p.   cm. — (Step into reading. A step 1 book.)
SUMMARY: Dinosaurs dance out of the book that a boy is reading and head for mischief.
ISBN 0-307-26200-6 (trade) — ISBN 0-375-99996-5 (lib. bdg.)
[1. Dinosaurs—Fiction. 2. Stories in rhyme.]   I. Lucas, Margeaux, ill. II. Title.
III. Series: Step into reading. Step 1 book.
PZ8.3.L966 Dan 2003   [E]—dc21   2002013407

Printed in the United States of America   30 29 28 27 26 25 24 23 22 21 20
First Random House Edition

STEP INTO READING®

STEP 1

DANCING DINOS

WITHDRAWN

By Sally Lucas
Illustrated by Margeaux Lucas

Random House 🏠 New York

Dinos dancing

on a stage.

Dinos dancing
off the page.

Dinos dancing
on the floor.

Dinos dancing

out the door.

Dinos swaying
down the hall.

Dinos playing
with a ball.

Tapping, clapping
with some toys.

Stamping, stomping,
making noise.

Dinos sliding
down the stairs.

Dinos gliding
by in pairs.

Dinos marching

through a room.

Dinos stomping–
boom, boom, boom.

Dinos munching
ham on rye.

Dinos crunching

pizza pie.

Dinos flipping
corn and peas.

Dinos flinging
gobs of cheese.

Dinos hopping
over pails.

Dinos mopping
with their tails.

Splishing, splashing
high and low.

Slipping, skipping…

Uh-oh!

Crashing, dashing
over chairs.

Jumping, jogging
up the stairs.

Dinos dancing

to a page.

Dinos dancing
on a stage.